The Doggonest
Christmas

The Doggonest Christmas

by Richard L. Stack

Illustrations by Charles W. Stack

The Doggonest Christmas

by Richard L. Stack

Illustrations by Charles W. Stack

Book design by Brown & Taylor, Dallas

Copyright 1988. Richard L. Stack

Printed in U.S.A. by Taylor Publishing Company, Dallas.

Distributed by Four Seasons Book Publishers

or contact Windmill Press
7609 Beaver Rd.
Glen Burnie, MD 21061

ISBN 0 — 9605400 — 6 — 7

Dedicated to Elly Mozikat Wargenau who really did feed the "doggies" in Davidsonville, Maryland, just as it says in the book.

Once upon a wintertime,
and not so very long ago,

way up north in the little
town of Bobsled,

lived a handsome young
dog named
Josh.

Josh was a lucky little dog, because he had the good fortune to live with a kind lady whose name was Miss Elly. She was known far and wide for her love of animals, and had a special place in her heart for dogs. She and Josh were the best of friends.

Many other dogs in Bobsled were not as lucky as Josh because they did not always have enough to eat. And so several times each week, Miss Elly would cook a big pot of dog food, made from her own special recipe. Then she would drive around Bobsled in her big blue car to feed the hungry dogs who waited for her by the side of the road. They always seemed to know when she was coming.

Josh went along with Miss Elly on these rides, and looked forward to seeing his many friends.

There were Bowser

and Fido,

and Mackie

and Rusty.

And there were Bobo

and Brownie,

and Blackie

and Willie.

Because Josh and his friends had different kinds of dogs in their families, they were called mongrels or mutts. Many people believed that they were worthless, but they were wonderful pets and gave much friendship and love to their owners.

Now, although Josh was a mutt, Miss Elly knew that he was not worthless. She believed that he would do something important with his life, but she was not sure what that would be.

One cold and windy night, Miss Elly sat reading by a cozy fire, with Josh stretched lazily across her lap. As he lay thinking how warm and comfortable he was, Josh heard Miss Elly ask him to look at something in her book.

He stood up on her lap and Miss Elly showed him a picture of the biggest dog he had ever seen.

"He is a St. Bernard," explained Miss Elly, "and he is trained to go out in the snow to rescue people who have lost their way."

Josh studied the picture carefully. The St. Bernard stood over a man who lay in the snow. The man was reaching for something which hung beneath the dog's big, furry head and Miss Elly could tell that Josh was curious.

"That is a keg hanging from his collar," she explained. "It is filled with something for the people to drink to keep warm."

"Wow, Oh Bow Wow," thought Josh, "how wonderful it must be for a dog to save a person's life. A St. Bernard must be the most important dog in the world." And it was at that moment that Josh decided what he wanted to do with his life.

"THAT IS WHAT I WANT TO BE! I AM GOING TO BE A ST. BERNARD!"

The little dog settled back across Miss Elly's lap again, but he was now much too excited to sleep. He was going to be a St. Bernard!

The next day, Josh was outside playing when he heard Miss Elly calling him. He ran into the house to see what she wanted, and found Miss Elly holding a bright red collar.

Hanging from the collar was a keg, just like the one worn by the St. Bernard in the book, but much smaller.

"Here is a present for you, Josh," said Miss Elly as she buckled the collar around his little neck. He was so excited that he found it hard to hold still.

Josh turned to look at himself in the tall mirror which stood on the floor. Miss Elly smiled when she saw how much Josh liked his present.

"Wow, Oh Bow Wow!" Josh yapped as he turned his head back and forth to look at himself from every side. And each time he moved his head, he could hear something sloshing around inside the keg. He wondered what it could be.

"I filled your keg with hot chocolate," explained Miss Elly.

It was the best present that she had ever given him, and he thanked her with lots of big kisses!

Josh could hardly wait to show his friends his present, and to tell them about his dream of becoming a St. Bernard. But when the other dogs saw him wearing his keg, they only laughed and made fun of him.

"You cannot be a St. Bernard," howled Fido.

"That is the silliest thing I ever heard," laughed Willie as he rolled over on his back and kicked his feet in the air.

"We will always be worthless mutts, and so will you," scolded Rusty through the long red hair which hung from his forehead.

Josh tried not to let them know that they had hurt his feelings, but they could tell that they had, and felt ashamed. After all, he was their friend, and they had not wanted to be mean to him.

"We are sorry," said Blackie, "but what you want is not possible. You cannot just decide to be a St. Bernard."

Josh did not answer his friends, and just walked slowly away. He would not let them spoil his dream.

When Josh returned home, Miss Elly could tell that the other dogs had made him sad. She stooped down and held him close to her.

"Josh," she said tenderly, "your friends are willing to ask far too little from life, and they expect you to think the same way. Many people are like that, too."

"It is not important whether you become a St. Bernard. What is important is that you do your best at whatever you try to do. As long as you do your best and believe in yourself, you can never be worthless."

When Miss Elly spoke to him this way, Josh understood how important he really was. From that day forward, Josh never left the house without his keg, which he wore proudly. And every morning, Miss Elly made sure that his keg was filled with fresh, delicious hot chocolate.

Now, this was wintertime, and in wintertime comes Christmas time. So one crisp afternoon, Josh and his friends took a walk around Bobsled to look at the beautiful Christmas decorations which people put up at this time of year.

The stores and shops had been decorated with red bows and evergreens, lights and all kinds of exciting ornaments. Just inside the window of the post office was a wonderful toy train that chugged around in a circle on a table. It puffed real smoke, and the dogs all crowded around to look.

Then up and down the streets they romped, their heads wagging back and forth almost as fast as their tails. There were so many sights to see, and they did not want to miss a thing.

Suddenly, they jolted to a stop, and their eyes grew wider than saucers. For coming down the snow-covered roadway was a wooden sled, with a tall Eskimo riding on the back. And out in front of the sled stretched a magnificent team of Huskies, pulling it along at breathtaking speed

This was the first time that any of the friends had ever seen a Husky, much less a whole team of them, and they were really excited.

"Mush, you Huskies!" shouted the Eskimo, and the Huskies pulled the sled even faster than before. The friends could see what fun the Huskies were having.

The Eskimo driver cracked his long whip and waved to the friends as the sled streaked past. Down the road it sped and just as suddenly as they had appeared, the Eskimo and his Huskies were gone from sight. Soon the friends could not even hear them anymore.

"Wow, Oh Bow Wow!" Willie was finally able to whisper. "I would give anything to be a Husky," he added, in a voice which sounded almost like a prayer.

The rest of the friends found it hard to speak, and just nodded their heads in agreement.

"Well, why can't you be Huskies," Josh finally spoke up, "if you really want to be?"

"Oh no, there he goes again," muttered Blackie. "That is just as silly as your thinking that you can become a St. Bernard."

"Don't you understand that we are just worthless mutts," added Mackie, "and so are you."

"I am not worthless, and I will be a St. Bernard some day," Josh answered. He remembered what Miss Elly had told him about believing in himself. He felt sad for his friends, for they did not dare to dream of being something better than they were.

Josh and his friends often thought about that afternoon, but soon their attention turned to the excitement of the Christmas season.

Christmas Eve arrived, and Josh had a wonderful time helping Miss Elly decorate their house. He watched as she hung two stockings by the chimney, a red one with a white toe for Josh, and a blue one for herself.

"Perfect," observed Miss Elly.

"Wow! Oh, Bow Wow!" Josh barked in agreement.

Miss Elly and Josh looked out the window, and saw that it had started to snow. "We will have a wonderful white Christmas," said Miss Elly.

The snow looked like a lot of fun, and Josh decided to go outside to play in it. After Miss Elly had buckled his collar and keg around his little neck, she opened the door for Josh. Down the steps he scampered and off he ran.

"Don't go too far," cautioned Miss Elly, because she saw how hard the snow was falling. Josh nodded his head to let her know that he understood, but soon Miss Elly could not see him anymore.

Josh discovered that the snow was even more fun than he thought it would be. First, he ran about, trying to catch the biggest snowflakes on the end of his tongue. Then he lay on his back making angel dogs in the ever-deepening snow. But as quickly as he made an angel dog, he noticed that it disappeared under a fresh mantle of white.

"Wow, Oh Bow Wow." "This snow is really getting deep," thought Josh. "Maybe this is what is called a blizzard!" And he was right, because a terrible winter storm was blanketing the little town of Bobsled!

Josh should have gone home at once, but he stopped and stood very still. He felt that something was just not right. He sniffed the wind deeply, and perked up his ears for any sound.

"What is wrong?" Josh wondered. And then, something deep within his senses told him someone was lost out in the snow!

Josh knew that there was not a moment to lose, and he started running even before he realized that his little legs were moving. With no thought for his own safety, out through the fields he ran and into the forest — faster than he had ever run before.

Josh stopped again and watched the snow swirling through the trees. He had never been in the woods when it was snowing, and nothing looked the same to him. The tall trees looked like giant white mushrooms and the bushes looked like big cotton balls. The stump over by the pond looked like a ... "WAIT A MINUTE," exclaimed Josh. "THAT IS NO STUMP! IT'S MOVING!"

Josh could feel his heart pounding deep within his chest as he bounded over to where the figure lay buried beneath the snow.

"What is under there?" he wondered. He sniffed at it cautiously, and realized that there was a person under the snow!

Frantically, Josh began pawing at the snowy mound, digging with all his might and throwing the snow behind him. Then he stopped digging, and he thought that his heart had stopped too. For there under the snow was a man, and Josh was afraid that he had not reached him in time.

Ever so carefully, Josh nudged the man with his nose, then again, a little harder this time. Slowly, the man began to move. Josh blinked his eyes and blinked them again. He could not believe what he was seeing, and thought that his mind must be playing tricks on him. But no, it was true.

There looking up at him was Santa Claus himself!

"You are Josh, that nice little dog who lives with Miss Elly," Santa was able to say. Santa's teeth chattered loudly when he spoke, and Josh could see that he was very cold.

"You know me?" Josh asked in amazement.

"Of course, I know you," replied Santa. "I received your Christmas letter, and your house was going to be one of my first stops this year."

Josh wondered what he could do to help Santa, and then he remembered his little keg.

"Here," said Josh, as he moved very close to Santa. "The hot chocolate in my keg will help you to be warm again."

Santa unfastened Josh's keg from his collar, and drank down every drop of the steamy hot chocolate. How good it was. Almost at once, Josh could see the rosy red color returning to Santa's cheeks and nose.

Santa was saved.

"Josh, you are truly a great rescue dog," said Santa, "even better than a St. Bernard."

"Wow, Oh Bow Wow!" said Josh, as he blushed with pride. "Me! Better than a St. Bernard!" How good Santa's words made him feel.

Josh wondered why Santa was out in the snow by himself. H
looked around for the sleigh and reindeer which surely must b
nearby, but they were nowhere to be seen.

"My reindeer caught colds while they were out playing reinde
games," Santa explained to Josh. "They are all tucked in bed back a
the North Pole, and will be fine."

"Without the reindeer to pull my big sleigh, I tried to deliver m
presents on foot. The terrible snowstorm surprised me in the wood

nd I lost my way.''

    Santa told Josh that he was really worried, because now he would
ot be able to deliver his presents. As Josh listened to Santa, he
hought of a plan that just might work. He asked Santa to return to
he North Pole and to wait for him there. Josh showed Santa the way
ut of the forest, and then he was off and running again. Soon he
as out of sight. Because he had faith in Josh, Santa started for home
ght away. But he wondered what the little dog had in mind.

Santa arrived back at the North Pole, and was just about to pull off his big black boots, when he heard Josh calling to him from outside his house. Santa rushed to the door and looked out. There on the snow-covered lawn were Josh, Bowser, Mackie and the rest of the friends.

"What is going on, Josh?" asked a very puzzled Santa Claus. Quickly, the little dog explained his plan.

"Santa, my friends have a dream of their own. They want to be Huskies. They can pull your sleigh. I just know they can!" And then the friends held their breath and waited for Santa to answer.

"Let them try," said Santa. "It is our only chance!"

"Wow! Oh, Bow Wow!" shouted the friends with glee, as they ran into the barn where Santa's big sleigh stood waiting. Quickly, they took their places and Santa's elves fastened them into the harnesses. How important the friends felt. Then Santa climbed up onto his sleigh.

"I want you to come along with us," Santa called to Josh. "Your friends do not know the way to go, and will need your help. With your keen senses, you will be perfect for the job."

"Wow, Oh, Bow Wow!" said Josh as he leaped up beside Santa. He was thrilled that he was going with them, and gave Santa lots of big kisses. "Ho! Ho! Ho!" Santa laughed and laughed.

Then, Santa took the reins in his strong hands and gave a reindeer command that was not like any that was ever before heard.

"ON BOWSER! ON FIDO! ON WILLIE AND MACKIE! ON BOBO! ON RUSTY! ON BROWNIE AND BLACKIE!"

But the big sleigh did not budge. Not one single inch!

"What is wrong?" asked Santa. "Is the sleigh too heavy for you?"

"No, Santa," Josh answered for the friends. "But, my friends want to be Huskies, not reindeer! So, if it would not be asking too much, could you please just tell them to 'Mush'?"

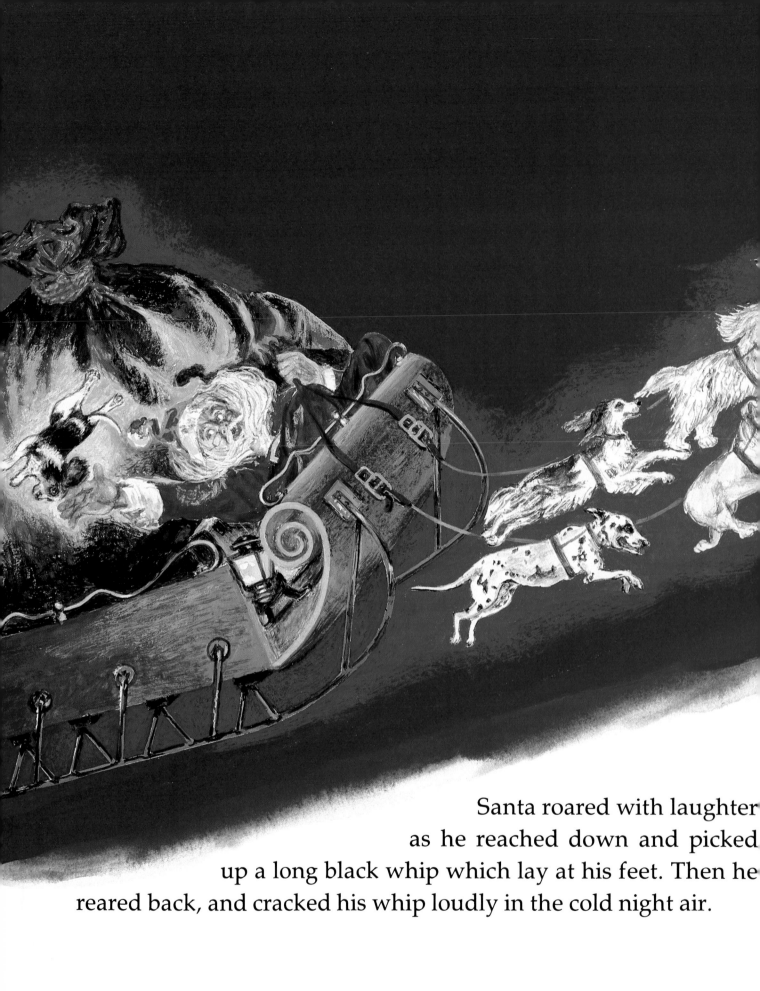

Santa roared with laughter
as he reached down and picked
up a long black whip which lay at his feet. Then he
reared back, and cracked his whip loudly in the cold night air.

"MUSH! MUSH, YOU HUSKIES!" shouted Santa. "MUSH!"

With that, the sleigh shot forward, as if from a giant cannon. Josh was almost thrown back out of the sleigh, and surely would have been, if Santa had not caught him just in time. And so, the long journey across the world had begun at last.

On Christmas morning, there was not a disappointed boy or girl to be found anywhere. All of Santa's toys and presents had been delivered, and everywhere there was joy and happiness.

In the little town of Bobsled, there were nine tired and weary dogs who slept right through Christmas day, much to the surprise of their owners. But Josh and his friends never had a happier Christmas, because their dreams had come true, and things would never again be the same for them. Now they understood that they could never be worthless, as long as they believed in themselves and did their very best at whatever they tried to do.

And over at the North Pole, Santa knelt down and said a prayer of thanks for wonderful people like Miss Elly and special dogs like Josh and his friends.

It was the doggonest Christmas ever!